THIS BOOK BELONGS TO

....

Published by Tate Publishing & Enterprises, LLC
127 E. Trade Center Terrace | Mustang, Oklahoma 73064 USA
1.888.361.9473 | www.tatepublishing.com

Tate Publishing is committed to excellence in the publishing industry. The company reflects the philosophy established by the founders, based on Psalm 68:11,
"The Lord gave the word and great was the company of those who published it."

Book design copyright © 2008 by Tate Publishing, LLC. All rights reserved.
Cover design & interior design by Elizabeth A. Mason
Illustrations by Benton Rudd

Published in the United States of America

ISBN: 978-1-60604-792-7
1. Juvenile Fiction: Family: Multigeneration
2. Youth & Children: Children: General
08.05.16

ISAAC

and the
Bah Family
Tree

written by:

Adrienne C. Wilson

TATE PUBLISHING & Enterprises

FOR HERMAN

There was a tree that stood alone in the Bah family's backyard. Thick, brown bark covered the trunk, while the gently swaying branches covered in leaves seemed to laugh from the wind's playful breeze.

Isaac Bah stood gazing at the tree. He walked around the thick trunk, running his fingers across the rough, brown bark. He placed his nose as close as possible so he could smell the earthy wood.

"Hello, Tree! How are you today?" said Isaac.

He placed his ear as close as he could to the branch so he wouldn't miss what the tree had to say. The tree didn't reply.

"Hello, Tree! Are you my family tree?"

But the tree still didn't speak. His friends at school had all talked about their family trees. Isaac was sure that this one was his. For a second, he thought he heard the tree laugh.

Isaac's Grandpa sat in the cozy, squeaking rocking chair peering curiously over his newspaper as he watched Isaac study the tree.

"Who are you talking to out there?" asked Grandpa, thinking Isaac had an imaginary friend.

"Nobody," Isaac replied. *Maybe this isn't my family tree after all,* he thought.

"Oh!" said Grandpa, as Isaac walked away from the tree.

Isaac decided to take a walk to the park where there were many trees. As he walked through the park he noticed several very large, small, and different trees. Isaac first tried talking to a Willow, but it said nothing and only wept when the wind blew. He tried speaking with an Oak, but the Oak, like the Willow, never spoke. The next tree he tried was a prickly Pine.

"Excuse me, Tree—are you my family tree?" Isaac asked.

For a moment there was silence, but then the tree finally started talking!

"Why no, I'm not your family tree. . ."

Then the tree burst into laughter. Out came Isaac's friend Kareem, tumbling from behind the Pine. Isaac felt hurt. He hoped that this was his family tree, but it was not.

"Look in your family's trunk. That's where I found my family tree," said Isaac's friend.

Isaac remembered his family had a trunk, and so he headed back to his house to find his tree in his family's trunk.

Grandpa Bah, who no longer sat in the cozy rocking chair, heard Isaac searching in the attic.

"What are you looking for up there?" he shouted.

"The family tree!" cried Isaac.

"But trees don't grow in attics!" Grandpa laughed, as he headed to his rocking chair in the living room.

Isaac continued to wonder about the places his friends had discovered their family trees. Convinced his tree was somewhere in the house, he took a photo album from the trunk and came down from the attic.

Grandpa Bah watched from the rocking chair as Isaac marched through the house.

"Any luck?" asked Grandpa.

"Not yet," Isaac replied.

Isaac didn't give up. He dug through shoeboxes in closets, cabinets under sinks, and every corner of the Bah house. Not knowing where else to look, he walked over to Grandpa Bah and told him about his problem. Grandpa gently pulled Isaac up into the rocking chair. With great care, he took the photo album from Isaac and opened the crackly old pages.

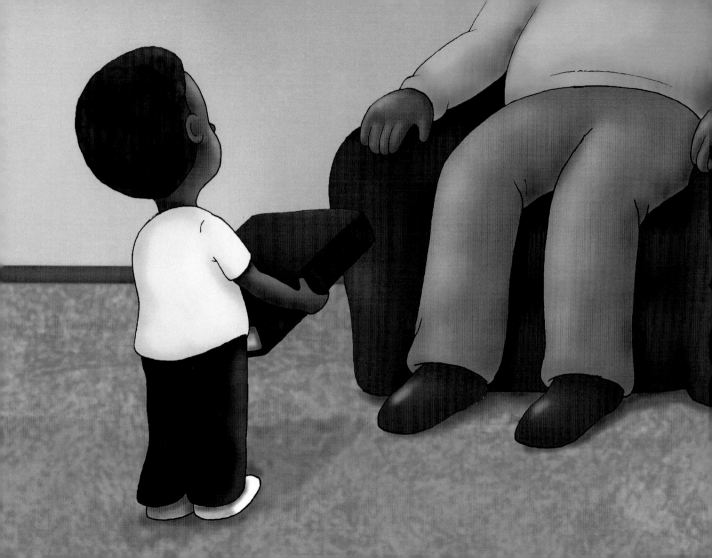

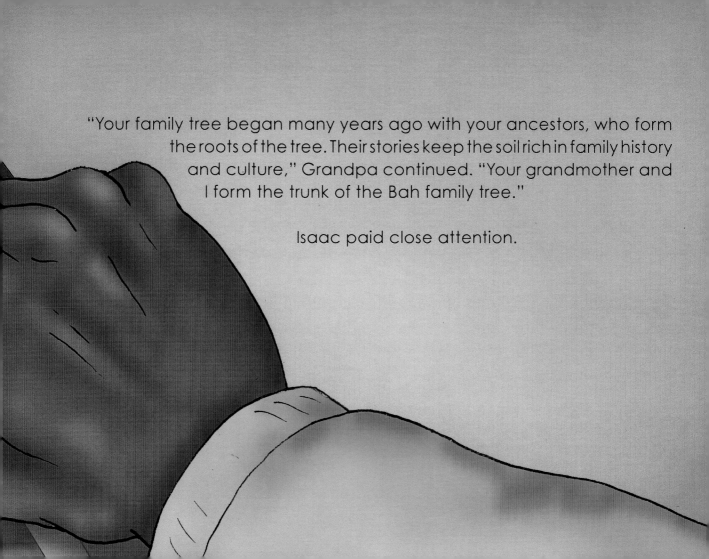

"Your family tree began many years ago with your ancestors, who form the roots of the tree. Their stories keep the soil rich in family history and culture," Grandpa continued. "Your grandmother and I form the trunk of the Bah family tree."

Isaac paid close attention.

"Your father and mother are branches. Extending from their branches are you and your sister," Grandpa said. "In time, many more branches will grow from you and Amelia—each unique in its own way."

Isaac's mother stopped cooking, grandmother stopped quilting, and father stopped snoozing to join them by the rocking chair. Amelia watched intensely from her playpen.

"Each part of the tree tells a story about our family. Many family members came from Africa, while some of them remained behind. A few were Native American or Indian from great tribes. Those ancestors worked hard at keeping our family strong."

Isaac sat amazed as the rest of the family smiled. Even Amelia giggled a little.

"So these pictures and stories make my family tree?" Isaac asked.

Grandpa stood up from the rocking chair. He took Grandmother's hand in his right hand and Isaac's father's hand in his left. Isaac's mother placed her hand in Isaac's father's hand and gently took Isaac's in her other. Isaac let go only to grab Amelia from her playpen. The Bah family raised their arms to the ceiling as high as they could reach.

"These branches are the strongest of any tree, for they are built of wisdom and strength," Grandpa said.

"And the leaves?" asked Isaac.

"The leaves," said Grandpa, "are filled with love."

There was a tree that stood alone in the Bah family backyard. Thick, brown bark covered the trunk, while the gently swaying branches covered in leaves seemed to laugh from the winds playful breeze. But the real family tree grew within the Bah family house.

e|LIVE

listen|imagine|view|experience

AUDIO BOOK DOWNLOAD INCLUDED WITH THIS BOOK!

In your hands you hold a complete digital entertainment package. Besides purchasing the paper version of this book, this book includes a free download of the audio version of this book. Simply use the code listed below when visiting our website. Once downloaded to your computer, you can listen to the book through your computer's speakers, burn it to an audio CD or save the file to your portable music device (such as Apple's popular iPod) and listen on the go!

How to get your free audio book digital download:

1. Visit www.tatepublishing.com and click on the e|LIVE logo on the home page.
2. Enter the following coupon code:
   c5cb-734b-1ab1-1f9e-e1e4-ca50-375d-9520
3. Download the audio book from your e|LIVE digital locker and begin enjoying your new digital entertainment package today!